D1387821

F
Darling, Kathy
The Easter Bunny's secret

The Easter Bunny's Secret

The Easter Bunny's Secret

By Kathy Darling

Pictures by Kelly Oechsli

GARRARD PUBLISHING COMPANY
CHAMPAIGN, ILLINOIS

The Easter Bunny's Secret

Spring Bunny watched her father
color an Easter egg.
"How do you make
the magic Easter egg paint?"
Spring wanted to know.
The Easter Bunny looked up.

"Only the Easter Bunny
knows the secret,"
he said to Spring.
"When I pick
a new Easter Bunny,
I will tell the secret."

"Who will be
the new Easter Bunny?"
Spring asked.
"I don't know yet,"
said her father.
He looked around at his helpers.

Some of the bunnies
were working very hard.
But the Easter Bunny's children
were not working at all.

One of Spring's brothers
was climbing a tree.
Her two sisters were having
a jelly bean fight.

The Easter Bunny
called to his children.
"We need more help
to paint Easter eggs,"
he said.
But only Spring
wanted to help.
"May I paint some eggs?"
she asked.
"Of course,"
said the Easter Bunny.
He looked in his basket.
All the eggs were gone.
"Get your basket,"
said the Easter Bunny.

"We will get more eggs."
Mother Bunny went with them.
Spring hopped down the path
with her mother and father.

Inside the hen house
were rows and rows of nests.
They were full of white eggs.
Carefully, Spring packed eggs
into her basket.

"One egg, two eggs,
three eggs, four,"
sang Spring.
"Five eggs, six eggs,
seven eggs more,"
sang the Easter Bunny.
Soon all their baskets
were full of eggs.
The bunnies went
down the path.
Hoppity hop. Hoppity hop.
The Easter Bunny
found a table for Spring.
He gave her
a jar of the magic paint.

Spring picked up an egg.
She painted polka dots
with the magic paint.
"That's a very pretty egg,"
said the Easter Bunny.
Spring was pleased.

She painted all the eggs
in her basket.
"Now that you are done,"
said her father,
"we will hide our eggs
for girls and boys
to find on Easter morning."

Spring and her father
went off to hide the eggs.
"Shall we hide one
by that rock?" he asked.
"I'll put one
here," said Spring.
"You hide the rest by yourself,"
said her father.
And he hopped away.

Soon only the polka-dot egg
was left. She hid it
in some tall grass
near pretty yellow flowers.
While Spring was hiding it,
she heard a funny little noise.

She looked around.
"What was that noise?"
she asked.
Then Spring heard mother call,
"It's time for lunch!"
Spring hopped home
singing a little song.

"Did you find good places
to hide your eggs?"
asked Mother Bunny.
"Yes," said Spring,
"it's fun to hide the eggs."

After lunch
mother went with Spring
to see where she had hidden
the polka-dot egg.

Spring looked through
the tall grass
near the yellow flowers.
But she could not find the egg.
"I know I put it here,"
Spring told her mother.

They looked some more,
but they could not find
the polka-dot egg.
"Let's look for another egg
you hid,"
said Mother Bunny.

They looked beside the tree.
But the egg
that Spring had put there
was gone.
"Don't cry, little one,"
said Mother Bunny.

"There are more painted eggs
that you can hide."
Spring and her mother
got two big baskets
full of colored eggs.

"I'll hide one
behind this bush,"
Spring said.
"That's a good place,"
said her mother.
"I am sure
you can find places
to hide all these eggs."
Then Mother Rabbit hopped away.
Spring hid all the eggs.
When she was through,
she sat down to rest.
A little noise
came from behind the bush
where she had hidden an egg.

"Someone is taking my eggs,"
Spring thought.
"I'll find out who it is."
She peeked behind the bush.
The egg she had hidden there
was gone!
She looked under the leaf.

That egg was not there.
Spring hopped fast
to her father.
She cried,
"Someone is taking our eggs.
Some that I just hid
are gone."

"Gone?" said her father.
"Who could be taking our eggs?
It's not Easter morning yet!"

None of the bunny helpers
knew who was taking the eggs.
"We must find out
where the eggs have gone,"
said the Easter Bunny.

Spring and her father
went off to look for the eggs.
"Maybe you forgot
where you put them,"
said the Easter Bunny.
"I know I hid one
behind this bush,"
said Spring.
"When I looked
it was not there."
Then they heard a little noise.
"Shhh," said her father.
"That's the same sound
I heard before,"
Spring whispered.

She and her father
peeked around the bush.
"Look!"
the Easter Bunny said.
"Someone broke the egg.
Here are bits of broken shell."

Spring began to cry.
"Someone broke my pretty egg."
Then the Easter Bunny
saw a yellow feather
near the broken shell.

"Let's look for something
with yellow feathers,"
he told Spring.
"Then we can find out
who is breaking
our pretty Easter eggs."

"Look!" Spring shouted.
"Here is an egg
that is not broken!"
While she was looking
at the egg,
it began to move.

Spring saw
a little hole in the egg.
The hole got bigger and bigger.

Then the egg broke in half.
A tiny chick
fell out of the shell.

It was wet and very tired.

The warm sunshine dried the chick.

Its yellow feathers puffed out.

"Peep, peep," went the baby chick.

Now Spring heard another noise.

"Cluck! Cluck!"

Spring looked under the bush.

She saw a mother hen.

The baby chick

ran to its mother.

"Baby chicks broke our eggs!"

Spring laughed.

"They were inside the shells."

She held one of the chicks.

It peeped softly.

"So that's where
some of your eggs went,"
said the Easter Bunny.
"No one was taking them.
Let's go back, little one,
and get more eggs to hide."

Everyone worked hard
painting and hiding more eggs.

Finally everything was ready
for Easter morning.
Spring sat down to rest.
"I'm tired,"
she said to her father.
The Easter Bunny
sat down beside her.

"The new Easter Bunny
is always tired
on Easter morning,"
he said.
Spring looked surprised.
"Yes," said her father,
"you are the new Easter Bunny!"

Then the Easter Bunny
whispered in Spring's ear,
"Now I can tell you
the secret of the magic
Easter egg paint!"